Agent Profile

TOP SECRET

Code name: BATTLE BOY BB005

Real name: Napoleon Augustus Smythe

Age: 11 years old

Assignment: Operation Battle Book

Controller: Professor Juanita Perdu

Duty: Operate as a Human Data-Collecting Device (HD-CD)

Directive: To spy on the past

Survival gear: SimulSkin, Battle Watch, Helping Hand, HoverVest, Boot Boosters, NukeBelt

First published 2010 in Pan by Pan Macmillan Australia Pty Limited
1 Market Street, Sydney

National Library of Australia
Cataloguing-in-Publication data:

Carter, Charlie.

Chariot charge / Charlie Carter.

9780330425889 (pbk.)

Carter, Charlie Battle boy ; 8.

For children.

A823.4

Designed by Russell Jeffery, Emigraph
Printed in Australia by McPherson's Printing Group

SPYING ON THE PAST

Chariot Charge

CHARLIE CARTER

ILLUSTRATED BY RUSSELL JEFFERY

PAN
Pan Macmillan Australia

CHAPTER ONE

'Can't I be a knight, or a king?' said Napoleon.

He stepped into the Tome Tower, grumbling to Professor Perdu, and walked over to the Battle Books.

Book 141 was rattling and rumbling, and whistling like a kettle on the boil.

'It's the Battle of Hastings,' he continued. '1066 and all that! William the Conqueror thumps Harold of Wessex. Total **mega-bash**. And I have to be a shepherd watching from the hillside.'

Napoleon tugged at the thick woollen, scratchy tunic he had to wear.

'Your mission in this Battle Book is to observe the battle only,' said Professor Perdu.

'But I'm an action boy. I'm ready for ANYTHING!'

There was a deafening explosion.

Napoleon was thrown right across the room.

He slammed into the wall –

KERSPLAT!

– and slid down it like a slugged slug.

Oooo! Ouch!

He lay dazed on the floor, covered in soot and debris. A siren was blaring, red lights flashing.

'What … what happened, Skin?' he said, sitting up slowly.

'Level … 7… Combustion Event,' Skin said in a broken voice

'Felt like a 10-plus to me.' Napoleon checked himself all over.

SimulSkin

Microcircuits

Nano-computer

Intelli-chips

Night Eyes (for infra-red vision)

Ear microphone

Eyes

Palms (LCD screens)

Eyes record information

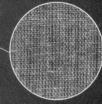

Eyes

Made from Kevlar and cloned spider web fibres

'You have minor bruising only,' said Skin.

'Thanks to you. You're the best skin ever, Skin.'

Napoleon had lost count of how many times his computerised, skin-coloured body armour had saved him from danger.

'Stay where you are, BB005,' Professor Perdu's voice came over the intercom. 'An emergency team is on its way to assess the situation.'

Her worried face was at the window of the Tome Tower.

Napoleon looked around him. The Tome Tower was in chaos. Control panels were blinking, circuits were exposed, wires were fizzing and sparking. The floor was covered in rubble, and Battle Books were scattered everywhere.

He saw a strange glow in the rubble, and looked closer.

'I repeat, BB005, stay where you are!'

There was a massive hole in the floor. Napoleon crawled to the edge – dodging wires and sparks – and peered over. The hole was easily two metres deep.

'Hey! There's a Battle Book down there,' he cried. 'And it's humming.'

'Don't go near it!' the professor shouted.

The Book was cracked, and a fine green mist was seeping from it. The hum was growing louder.

'I can't quite read its number,' said Napoleon, leaning further over the hole. 'Hang on. It's No. 2 —'

There was a tearing sound and the crack in the book suddenly opened wide.

The hum became a **ROAR**.

'WHOA!' shouted Napoleon as the ground shuddered and shook. 'I'm going to fall …'

And he toppled into the hole.

CHAPTER TWO

'HELP!'

The wind was screaming in Napoleon's ears, and he had to shield his eyes.

He could feel the skin on his face stretching with speed.

This was high velocity time travel.

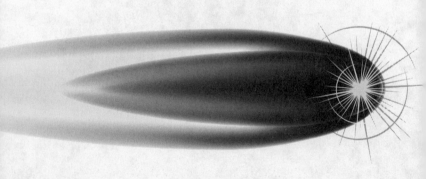

'Why are we going so super fast, Skin? And *where* are we going?' he shouted.

'Impossible to say. The GC-Locator was damaged in the explosion. Co-ordinates do not compute. But I estimate that we have travelled more than two thousand years already.'

'It feels like we're **zooming** through history. We'll be back with the cavemen soon.'

'Limited visual data coming into view now.'

Napoleon could just make out snow-capped mountains far below. But he soon whizzed passed them.

'Man-made structures visible in Sector 5F,' said Skin.

A grid system flashed across Napoleon's

COORDINATES: 34°35'N, 36°31'E
RANGE: 1800 m

eyes. He could see a vast city with massive stone walls.

'Zeroing in for micro-inspection,' said Skin, and then paused to analyse the data. 'Ancient architecture. Possible period: 1400–1100 BC. Possible area: somewhere between Egypt and the Black Sea.'

A moment later, a large body of water appeared in the distance.

'That is the Mediterranean Sea,' said Skin. 'Geographic area now identified as Syria. Historical period still uncertain.'

'Professor?' said Napoleon. 'Can you hear me? I don't think we're going to the Battle of Hastings.'

'Transmission down,' said Skin. 'Attempting activation of manual backup.'

Suddenly they broke through the mist. A rocky desert spread out below.

'Are we stopping?' said Napoleon.

'Affirmative,' Skin replied. 'Descending at maximum rate.'

The ground was **looming** up at Napoleon.

'We usually slow down a bit to stop, Skin,' said Napoleon anxiously.

'Impossible', said Skin. 'Boot Boosters not responding, and HoverVest operating only in secondary mode.'

'And I don't usually land on rocks either,' Napoleon shouted, staring at the ground below.

'The rocks are hard but round,' said Skin. 'Recommend rolling over the top of them, if possible.'

'Great advice, Skin,' said Napoleon as he rocketed towards the ground.

At the very last moment the Boot Boosters gave a spurt and the HoverVest found a few extra gyroscopic revs. This broke Napoleon's impact a little. He skimmed across the top of the rocks, but then made serious contact.

'**Youch!**

Yikes!

Yipes!'

He bumped and thumped over the rocks for at least twenty metres.

When he finally stopped, Napoleon was hurting all over. He stood up slowly and looked around.

Desert.

Hot, dry rocky desert as far as he could see.

The sun burned through his skin and his eyes ached with the glare.

'Why have we landed here, Skin? There's nothing in sight.'

'The GC-Locator is not 100 percent functional,' said Skin.

'Is anything working?'

'The explosion caused multiple system failures. But circuits will self-repair in time. Boot Boosters and HoverVest have almost repaired themselves, and software programs are rebooting.'

'Good,' said Napoleon. 'Let's find some shade. It's hot!'

He started heading for a big boulder he had spied about 500 metres away.

He trudged slowly across the flat stony ground.

'Any chance of a camel, Skin?' he asked. 'Or a paraglider?'

'Negative, BB,' said Skin. 'Feet are the only available means of transport at present.'

At about 400 metres from the boulder, Napoleon saw a dust cloud rising in the distance. A desert storm?

At 300 metres, he heard a rumble. Thunder?

At 200 metres, he felt the ground tremble. An earthquake? A stampede of angry camels?

At 100 metres, Skin gave a warning beep. 'Unidentified danger approaches.'

The dust cloud now filled the sky, blocking out the sun, while the ground shook fiercely under Napoleon's feet.

He stared ahead, and what he saw made his heart miss a beat.

'Are they what I think they are?' he said.

'Affirmative. Danger identified as chariots. Possibly Egyptian, but more likely . . .'

But Napoleon wasn't listening. He was running as fast as he could to the boulder.

CHAPTER THREE

Napoleon threw himself behind the big rock, gasping for breath.

An army of chariots was thundering across the desert. A deafening roar of men and horses.

Skin's nano-computers whirred, recording and assessing the data.

'Updating analysis. The chariots are not Egyptian. They are Hittite – of the three-man type – powerful war machines, but heavy and hard to manoeuvre.'

'There must be thousands of them,' said Napoleon.

'Correct. Three thousand is an approximate estimate.'

'Where are they going?'

'To a battle, of course.'

'But which battle?'

'Possibilities have been narrowed to four at this stage, BB005. Recommend the following course of action to determine exactly which battle: follow them.'

'But how? I haven't even got a donkey.'

'Carts carrying food and weapon supplies will follow soon. They are larger and slower. Be ready to board one.'

Skin was right. Behind the mass of charging chariots, a smaller group of carts trundled at a less hurried pace.

'HoverVest activated,' said Skin as the last cart passed.

Napoleon lifted from the ground.

'Boot Boosters operative in

4 . . .

3 . . .

2 . . .'

He shot off, and in no time at all had caught up to the last cart. The driver was cracking his whip and urging his horses through the dust.

Napoleon flew in behind the cart and edged closer until he was hovering above the back half.

It was full of swords, spears, helmets, shields and arrows. The plan was to float down, land quietly and hide among the weapons.

But then Skin gave a warning beep. 'HoverVest malfunctioning. Unable to . . .'

The HoverVest fizzed and spluttered. Napoleon plunged into the cart. The weapons clanged and clattered.

The driver turned around, but Napoleon burrowed quickly under some shields.

'PHEW! That was close,' he whispered to Skin. 'He looks mean, that driver.'

Skin was busy assessing the weapons.

'These are definitely Hittite. Notice the curve of the swords, the cone shape of the helmets, the shape of the arrow heads, and the patterns engraved on the shields. Excellent data, BB005.'

Data, frittata, thought Napoleon as the cart crashed along and he was bashed and bumped, jabbed and stabbed by all the arrows, spears, swords and daggers.

After what seemed like forever, the cart slowed down and stopped.

Napoleon crawled from under the shields and peeped about.

They were outside an ancient city, its massive walls rising from the desert. The other carts were there, too, along with thousands of chariots.

'City identified,' said Skin. 'It is Kadesh, the southern capitol of the Hittite Empire. There should be a river nearby.'

Napoleon could see it shimmering in the sun.

'That is the Orontes River,' Skin continued. 'This is where two great empires meet – Hittite and Egyptian. And they are about to fight for who controls this area.'

'So you know what Battle Book we're in?' said Napoleon.

'Of course. This is Book 214. It contains the Battle of Kadesh in 1274 BC, the greatest chariot clash in history – between the Hittites and Egyptians. More than six thousand chariots in mortal combat.'

'That's a crowd of chariots,' said Napoleon. 'And the Hittites look ready for battle.'

They were lined up in battle formation outside the walls of Kadesh. A tall warrior in a bright red chariot was riding back and forth in front of them.

'That is King Muwatalli,' said Skin, 'a fearless fighter.' The king's bronze armour and helmet shone like gold in the sun.

'Where are the Egyptians?'

'Their arrival is imminent, BB,' said Skin. 'They approach from the south.'

Napoleon saw a cloud of dust rising. Then, he felt the ground rumble.

'The Egyptians are led by one of the greatest pharaohs of all time,' Skin said. 'Ramses II. He has sworn to teach the Hittites a lesson and destroy the city of Kadesh.'

Suddenly Napoleon's Battle Watch flashed and beeped, and Professor Perdu's voice crackled with static.

'BB005. Are you okay?'

'I'm fine, Prof. We're in Book 214.'

'I know. Which is both good news and bad news.'

'How bad is bad?' said Napoleon. 'Is it "not too bad", or "couldn't be more bad" bad?'

'Somewhere in between,' said the professor. 'Book 214 is seriously damaged. We can't send an Exit Beam until we repair the cracks, and that's going to take some time.'

'So the good news must be really really good,' said Napoleon, 'to make me feel better about the chance of being STUCK HERE FOREVER!'

'Well, if you have to be stuck in a Battle Book,' said the professor, 'you couldn't be in a better one.'

'That's it?' said Napoleon. 'That's my good news?'

'There are two great mysteries of history in this book,' said the professor. 'Now you have a chance to solve both of them.'

'Two mysteries,' said Napoleon. 'So it's a two-for-one Battle Book.'

'Exactly, and both mysteries have intrigued historians through the ages because they are so —'

But Napoleon didn't hear anymore.

A rough hand had clamped down on his shoulder.

CHAPTER FOUR

'**You good-for-nothing scoundrel!**'

A Hittite soldier glared at Napoleon.

'Stealing the king's weapons?' He hauled Napoleon to his feet. 'You'll hang for this.'

Napoleon twisted and squirmed, and managed to wriggle free.

He leaped over the edge of the cart and ran for his life.

'**Thief!**' the soldier shouted, chasing after Napoleon. '**Stop him!**'

'Are you still receiving me, BB005?' asked Professor Perdu, her voice even more crackly than before. 'You sound distracted.'

'Yeah,' Napoleon yelled as he ran. 'I'm a bit caught up right now . . .'

'But I know you want to hear about the two mysteries,' continued the professor.

Napoleon glanced over his shoulder. Several soldiers were after him now.

'The first is about the battle itself: Who won it?' said the professor.

'But I thought we knew that already?' puffed Napoleon. The soldiers were firing arrows and throwing spears. 'Isn't it written down in history?'

'Yes. Twice, in fact. The Hittites recorded the battle on clay tablets, and the

Egyptians put it on papyrus. Trouble is, both sides claim victory.'

'My money's on the Hittites,' said Napoleon as a spear shot past his ear. 'They seem pretty bloodthirsty to me. But let me guess: you want me to watch the battle and find out who *really* won.'

'Precisely,' said the professor. 'That shouldn't be too hard. It's probably one of your easiest missions yet.'

A swarm of arrows buzzed over Napoleon's head.

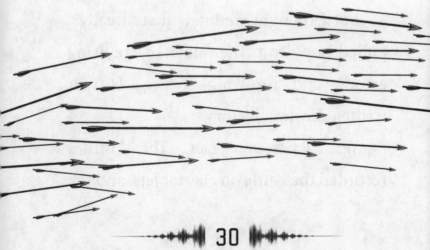

'Skin,' said Napoleon. 'Any time you want to **DO SOMETHING**.'

'HoverVest and Boot Boosters still malfunctioning, BB. But the auto-repair system is working on the problem.'

'Can't you hurry it up?' Napoleon said.

'What was that, BB?' asked the professor, her voice full of static.

'Nothing, Prof,' said Napoleon. 'What about the other mystery?'

'Prince Terrepas died at the Battle of Kadesh and was buried somewhere in the city. But his tomb has never been found.'

'And we want to find it because — ?'

'Because it's full of treasure – there's a mountain of Hittite gold.'

'Gold! I like the sound of that.'

'According to legend, there's a full-size chariot made of pure gold, and — '

'Yeah. They like their chariots. There's one after me **right now**.'

He could see the snarling faces of the Hittite soldiers as they came closer and closer.

'What did you say, BB?'

'I said, I'll get onto looking for that tomb **right now**.'

'Good work, BB. And I'll get onto fixing the Exit Beam.'

'Excellent example of a Hittite war chariot,' said Skin. 'Notice the swords projecting from the wheels. A most effective addition.'

Napoleon could hear the swishing of the swords as they spun their deadly circles.

He was running parallel to the city wall, searching for an alcove or a hole, anywhere to hide from the chariot.

'SKIN! What do I do?'

'One suggestion is . . .'

Napoleon didn't hear the rest. Peering behind him while running as fast as he could, he tripped on a rock and went headfirst into the desert gravel, tumbling over and over.

His head aching, he glanced up from the ground to see the chariot bearing down him on.

Any moment now he would be **sliced** and **diced**!

Then he noticed a crack at the base of the city wall. It was no more than forty centimetres high, and maybe a metre and a half long. But that was enough, Napoleon reckoned, if he held his breath and pulled in his tummy.

He rolled sideways and squeezed under the crack just as the chariot thundered past. The tip of one spinning sword passed within millimetres of his face.

'That's what I call a close shave,' he said.

He was safe . . . for the moment.

CHAPTER FIVE

Napoleon was pressed to the ground, his arms pinned beside him.

The air was hot and stale.

A spider ran over his hand and a scorpion scuttled past his face.

He shuddered. He didn't like small spaces. Or creatures starting with 'S'. They made him shiver and shake.

'Heart is racing dangerously, BB,' said Skin. 'Breathe in. And out. Try to think calm thoughts.'

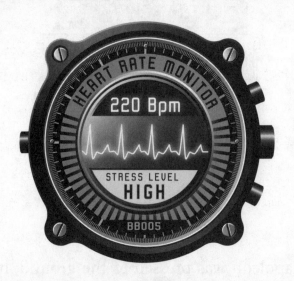

'I'll be calmer when I can get out of here, Skin,' said Napoleon. 'Do you think it's safe to leave yet?'

'No. You must go further under the wall, out of their reach.'

Napoleon gulped. 'Are you sure there's no other way?'

'Level of certainty one hundred per cent. My Sonic Beam indicates that the crack widens.'

Skin was right. It was a tight squeeze at first; Napoleon had to wriggle and squirm. But just when he thought he couldn't go any further, the ground fell away steeply beneath him, and he tumbled into a deep cavern.

Now he was in total darkness.

'I suppose the Night Eyes were damaged in the explosion?'

'Affirmative. However, they are still operating in Safety Mode. That will give limited vision. Activating now.'

The darkness faded to a deep soupy grey. Napoleon peered into it and slowly realised that he was sitting next to … a grinning skull.

'**AAAHHH!**'

He jumped up and screamed, knocking into another skeleton.

It rattled into a heap on the ground.

He was surrounded by skeletons.

Some sat in dusty chairs, others lay on stone slabs.

'Area identified as Hittite burial chamber,' said Skin.

'So it's full of **really dead people**!' said Napoleon. 'Get me out of here.'

'Assessing exit situation now.'

Skin scanned the chamber with his Sonic Beam. Nothing showed up on the first and second passes, and Skin gave out a long line of negative beeps. But at the end of the third sweep, Napoleon heard the positive hum that meant something had been found.

Sonic Beam: see with your ears

'Possible exit passage, Sector K8.'

Napoleon stared through a grid pattern and quickly located that sector. He identified what looked like a door cut into the stone wall.

He fumbled slowly through the dark, bumping into more skeletons.

'Whoops, sorry,' he said. 'I'm just leaving.'

Finally, the door was in front of him. A long skeleton was hanging from it, a bony right hand held out in a kind of gruesome greeting.

He reached out and grasped the skeleton's hand. 'Pleased to meet you, Bony,' he said.

The skull's jaw fell open in an ugly laugh, a swarm of bats flew out, and . . .

Napoleon dropped through the floor.

He fell onto a stone slide that was steep and smooth.

He shot through a leather flap, and bounced across a marble floor, stopping at the foot of a statue that was part-man, part-lion, part-eagle and all angry.

It glowered down at Napoleon.

'You are in the temple of Zimurg, a little known but most feared Hittite god,' said Skin. 'And you are not alone.'

A tall, thin boy stepped from behind a curtain. He was dressed in a silver caftan and golden sandals, and was wearing a golden cone-shaped cap on his head.

'I thought I heard something,' he said, staring at Napoleon. Skin translated the boy's words from Hittite. 'You should have been here ages ago.'

'Sorry,' said Napoleon. 'I got delayed. There was a chariot jam outside the city.' His words came out in Hittite, but they were slow and broken; Skin seemed to be having trouble.

Translator functioning at 75% capacity:
Words may be v e r y
s l o w ...

'You don't speak very well,' said the boy. 'But otherwise you'll do for the job, I suppose.'

'The job?' Napoleon looked confused.

'Didn't they tell you what you'd be doing?' said the boy.

'Probably,' said Napoleon, 'but I've forgotten. Could you tell me again, please?'

The Hittite Daily

WANTED
TEMPLE BOY
PREVIOUS TEMPLE
EXPERIENCE NOT
NECESSARY.

APPLY TO
ORACLE BOY

The boy sighed. 'Why do they always send me the stupid ones? You'll be training for the position of Temple Boy. I'm the Supreme Receiver of Oracles and I'll be in charge of you. My name is Haprall, but you can call me Master Haprall. Do you think you can keep that much in your head?'

'I'll try, Hap – sorry, *Master* Haprall. When do I start this, er, job.'

'Right now. Is there any reason why you can't?'

'I really wanted to watch the battle.'

'Everyone in Kadesh will watch the battle. It's our duty as good Hittites. That's where I was heading when you dropped in.'

He kicked Napoleon.

'Up you get, boy! The battle will be over before we get there at the speed you move. It won't take long for our great King Muwatalli to beat that puffed up pharaoh.'

Haprall marched off in long strides. Napoleon hurried after him.

'What is your name?' said Haprall. 'You will, of course, just be "boy" to me. But I need your name for the records.'

'Skin, I need a Hittite name,' Napoleon said through the thought channel. 'Quickly.'

Skin's nano-computers buzzed. But they were not working as fast as usual either.

'I said your name, boy. What is it? Or have you forgotten that as well?'

'Ikbresh,' Napoleon blurted out at last.

'Really?' Haprall stopped and turned around. 'Ikbresh! He smiled. 'That's perfect!'

'It is?' said Napoleon.

'You must know that *Ikbresh* means *battle* in Hittite,' said the boy. 'And that's a good omen. You are here to bring us luck in our battle against the pharaoh. And I know what I'll call you – Battle Boy!'

He slapped Napoleon on the back. 'I smell victory. Come, Battle Boy. Let us watch this fight to end all fights!'

CHAPTER SIX

Haprall led Napoleon to the top of the city walls. From there they could see right over the battlefield, down to the River Orontes.

The battle had started. Thousands of chariots were racing back and forth, clashing and smashing in a fury of wood, leather, metal and horseflesh.

The walls of Kadesh were crowded with citizens. They were yelling and cheering because the Hittites were winning.

'The pharaoh has fallen for the king's trap!' Haprall shouted.

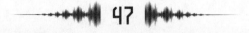

'The Hittite king, Muwatalli, hid most of his chariots,' explained Skin, 'so Ramses thought he would have an easy victory. Muwatalli has sprung his trap and Ramses is now in trouble.'

'Luck is on our side, too,' Haprall boasted loudly. 'The gods have sent us a new temple boy whose name means "battle".' He pushed Napoleon forward for all to see.

The High Priest of the Temple was most pleased to hear this. 'It is a good sign,' he said. 'And look, the pharaoh's men are running away already.'

It was true. Many of the Egyptians were fleeing, chased by the Hittites. As for Ramses, he was surrounded by hundreds of enemy chariots, unable to move.

'Victory will soon be ours,' cried the citizens of Kadesh.

But Ramses was fighting hard. He saw an escape route, pulled his chariot around and raced away.

'Run like a frightened dog!' the High Priest yelled.

The crowd cheered with him.

'Watch closely, BB,' said Skin. 'Ramses is about to play his trick.'

Napoleon saw the Egyptian chariots scattering in all directions.

The Hittites had to split their forces to chase them.

'The Egyptian chariots are much lighter and faster,' Skin explained. 'They have only two men on board, not three, and they can easily out-manoeuvre the heavier Hittite machines.'

The Egyptian chariots let the Hittites almost catch them, but then they turned sharply and wheeled around so that now they were chasing the Hittites.

The crowd roared in disbelief.

'And the Egyptians have new weapons as well,' Skin added. 'Ramses has equipped his army with new bows and arrows, better battleaxes, and a long curved sword called the khopesh. It is a deadly weapon. And, look! There is the mighty pharaoh himself.'

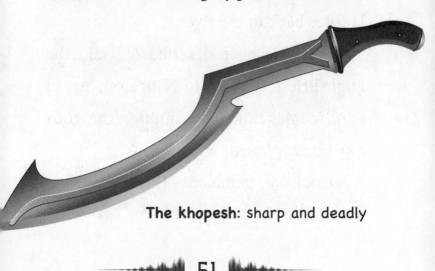

The khopesh: sharp and deadly

Ramses rode into view beneath the walls of Kadesh. He was dressed in golden armour with a blue cloak that flowed behind like giant wings. His chariot was bright blue.

The people of Kadesh booed and hissed. But Ramses slashed his sword in the air, called to his men and charged into battle.

They followed at once, and this time their force was so great that it pushed the Hittites back to the river.

'The gods have deserted us,' said the High Priest, turning to Napoleon. 'An ill wind circles our great empire. The gods must be appeased.'

Napoleon trembled. The priest was giving him the evil eye. 'I know,' Napoleon said. 'Let's all shout out "SORRY" really loudly. Then the gods will know it wasn't us.'

'There is only one way to satisfy the gods,' said the High Priest, narrowing his eyes. 'Yes, I see now. That is why they have sent us one whose name means *battle* – to sacrifice for victory!'

He moved towards Napoleon.

'No, I don't think that's right,' said Napoleon. 'My mum says there are always two sides to every story. The gods didn't send me. Honest. I'm here by accident.'

'There is no such thing as accident,' the priest said. 'The gods control everything, and they are hungry.'

He drew his dagger and grabbed at Napoleon. But Haprall stepped in his path.

'Most High and Mighty One. I implore

you. The boy brings luck, not misfortune.'

'Out of my way, Oracle Boy!' The High Priest pressed his dagger against Haprall's throat. 'Or the gods will have two sacrifices.'

The High Priest tightened his grip on the dagger. 'Look before you!' he shouted to the crowd. 'Is this a scene of victory?'

CHAPTER SEVEN

Everyone on the city walls stared in horror. Hittite chariots were overturned in the river, twisted and buckled. Hittite soldiers were fleeing, some on foot, others trying to swim.

'It's the end!' someone cried.

'No. WAIT!' cried another voice.

A horde of Hittite chariots suddenly poured onto the battlefield and attacked the Egyptians with a burst of fury.

'The Hittite king kept them hidden,' said Skin. 'Brilliant military tactics. I estimate approximately one thousand chariots.'

'King Muwatalli has outsmarted the pharaoh!' the people of Kadesh cheered.

'Yes!' Haprall shouted, the priest's dagger pressing hard on his throat. 'And Battle Boy's luck has not deserted us.'

'That's right,' Napoleon added, his eyes pleading with the priest. 'I'm lucky, lucky, lucky. You won't need any sacrifices now.'

The High Priest lowered his dagger.

'You'd better hope your luck remains. The gods never forget.'

Napoleon heaved a sigh of relief, and moved away with Haprall.

'Thanks,' he said when they were alone. 'You saved my life.'

'The High Priest is a bloodthirsty devil,' said Haprall. 'He loves a sacrifice more than anything. But come. There is still a battle to win.'

The day was long and the battle furious.

Soldiers from both sides charged in their chariots until they could charge no more.

By mid-afternoon, the battlefield was covered in bodies and broken chariots.

Muwatalli

Ramses

The two kings faced each, both proud and defiant.

But there could be only one victor.

Ramses surveyed his tired troops. He knew they could not withstand another chariot charge from the Hittites.

He called off his forces, gathered them together, and rode from the battlefield.

The exhausted Hittites watched them leave.

King Muwatalli rode around the outside of Kadesh calling to his people. 'Ramses came to destroy our great city. But we sent him off like a dog with his tail between his legs. Victory is ours!'

'Technically, that is incorrect,' said Skin. 'Neither side won this battle. It is what they call a stalemate.'

But the people of Kadesh didn't care. They hugged and laughed and danced in the streets.

Haprall cheered louder than anyone, and held up Napoleon for all to see. 'I said he would bring luck to us.'

He did five somersaults in a row, kissed a whole bunch of girls, and danced down the street with an old woman.

'This is the happiest day of my life. We have beaten the pharaoh. We are free.'

But then suddenly a deep gong

boomed

across the city.

The gong's sad sound froze the smile on every face.

'One of our great lords has perished in the battle,' said Haprall. 'But who? Who has died?'

'Prince Terrepas,' someone moaned, and cries of despair swept through the city.

'One of our greatest princes,' said Haprall, tears streaming down his face. 'The king's son.' He wiped his tears. 'The time for joy is over. We must prepare to send this great warrior to the Land of Darkness.'

CHAPTER EIGHT

The people of Kadesh were in mourning.

They wept. They beat their chests and tore out their hair. They stood in the street, heads hung low, waiting for the funeral procession that would take Prince Terrepas to his tomb.

At the royal palace, King Muwatalli and his queen were dressed in black robes. So too were the lords and ladies, all carrying gifts for the prince to take to his tomb.

The body of Terrepas was in a jewel-encrusted casket laid out on a silver carriage. It was hitched to a golden chariot pulled by two pure black horses, the prince's favourite steeds. They would take him on his final journey to the Land of Darkness.

Napoleon stared in awe at the treasure heaped around the prince.

'It's true,' he whispered to Skin. 'All the riches. The golden chariot, the jewelled casket, it's all here.'

'Correct,' said Skin. 'And none of it has been seen since the burial.'

'We'll soon change that.' Professor Perdu was back, her voice much clearer than before. 'As long as you stay with the funeral procession, BB005, and record the co-ordinates of the tomb.'

'I'll do my best, Prof. But what about the Exit Beam? Is it fixed yet?'

'Almost. I'm working as fast as I can.'

Napoleon glanced around at all the mourners. He'd be glad to get away from this miserable place.

Haprall was crying like everyone else. His head was shaved.

'He was the best of princes,' said Haprall. 'Always so kind to me. I will miss him dearly.'

Napoleon saw the High Priest, too. He was in charge of the funeral procession.

'Don't worry, Haprall,' the priest said with a sneer. 'I have arranged for you to stay with Prince Terrepas. You and your new friend.'

'How can we stay with the prince?' said Napoleon. 'He's going to his tomb.'

'Yes,' said the High Priest, his mouth twisted cruelly. 'And so are you.'

'What?' Napoleon backed away.

'Don't be afraid, Battle Boy,' said Haprall. We are the Chosen Ones. It is a great honour. We will journey with Prince Terrepas to the Land of Darkness.'

LAND OF DARKNESS

Napoleon shook his head. 'No thanks. I like it right here in the Land of Lightness.'

'You have earned this honour,' said the High Priest. He held up a razor. 'Shave your head and you'll be ready for the journey.' He lunged at Napoleon.

'I'm too young to shave!' shouted Napoleon, leaping out of the priest's way.

Several temple workers grabbed at him, but he sprang onto a pedestal and then climbed higher onto a shelf. The workers climbed after him.

'Where's that Exit Beam, Skin? I need it now like never before.'

'Exit Beam being prepared,' said Skin. 'Warning, however: Strength of beam is low, quality inferior. Omega Phase not fully engaged.'

Napoleon didn't even hear the warning, the High Priest was shouting so loudly. **'Seize him, you fools!'**

Two temple workers had climbed onto the shelf on either side of Napoleon and were edging towards him. The High Priest waited below. 'Don't be foolish, boy,' he said. 'This is your fate.'

That was when the Exit Beam appeared. It flickered at first and then shone brightly, right next to the High Priest. With the two temple workers only metres from Napoleon, he grinned down at the priest.

'Catch me if you can,' he said and dived from the shelf into the beam.

The High Priest stumbled out of the way and stared in amazement as Napoleon plummeted towards him and then vanished into thin air.

CHAPTER NINE

As Napoleon tumbled into the Exit Beam, he was still worrying about Haprall.

'Anxiety levels high, BB,' said Skin. 'It was common practice in ancient times for the living to be buried with the dead. Haprall believes he is going on a journey with a great warrior.'

'But he's not, is he?' said Napoleon. 'He's going to die in that tomb. I should have done something. And now it's too late.'

'Lateness is a relative concept,' said Skin.

'What do you mean?' Napoleon replied as he rocketed upwards. He was on his way into the future, to Professor Perdu and the Special Reading room.

'"Too late" implies the passing of time,' said Skin, 'but the Exit beam is not functioning fully. We are trapped in the Timeless Zone. We are not moving forwards, or backwards.'

Napoleon suddenly realised that he was floating above the city of Kadesh, trapped in a kind of time balloon.

It was a strange feeling. He could see the Hittites, but they couldn't see him. He was invisible inside the Exit Beam.

'What do we do?'

'We do nothing,' said Skin. 'We wait. We will float down eventually. And that is when we can try to exit again. The professor is still attempting to fix the beam.'

From above the city Napoleon could see the funeral procession filing along the streets. When it came to the city gates it went through them and out into the countryside.

'Aha!' said Professor Perdu. 'Now we know why Prince Terrepas's tomb was never found. Archaeologists have been searching in the wrong place. It is not in the city at all. It is somewhere beyond the walls.'

The procession wound its way into the countryside, like a long slithering snake.

'We are following them,' said Napoleon.

'Correct,' said Skin. 'We are leaving the Timeless Zone. And we are descending.'

When the procession was several kilometres from the city, they came to a stone building that looked like a small pyramid.

King Muwatalli held up his hand and everyone stopped.

'This structure is called a ziggurat,' said Skin. 'The Hittites built many of these.'

Napoleon was close enough now to clearly see the stepped walls of the ziggurat. Soon he was directly above the tomb. A moment later he was on the ground. The Exit Beam glowed a deep yellow for a few seconds and then faded.

'OK, BB005,' said the professor. 'Your bodily form has been restored. You are back in the Hittite world and fully visible. Have you recorded the coordinates for the tomb?'

TOMB
CO-ORDINATES:
34° 35' 12" N
36° 31' 15" W

BB005

Napoleon checked his Battle Watch. 'Roger that.'

'Good. And I've worked out what's wrong with the Exit Beam, so we should have you away from there soon.'

'No hurry, Prof,' said Napoleon, sneaking around the side of the ziggurat. 'There's still one thing I want to do.'

'No, BB005!' Professor Perdu shouted.

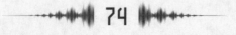

'Both mission objectives have been accomplished. It is time to leave. The Exit Beam is almost ready.'

'Well keep it on the boil,' Napoleon said as he quickly slipped into the crowd that had formed in front of the ziggurat. He was soon at the entrance to the tomb.

He saw Haprall and called out. But the Hittite boy didn't hear him. Napoleon blended into the mourners and kept walking.

It was dark inside the tomb. Flickering oil lamps cast dancing shadows on the walls and the air was thick with incense. The High Priest wailed and moaned while his helpers chanted a funeral song as the procession moved through the narrow tunnels towards the prince's final resting place.

When Napoleon arrived at the main chamber, he stopped and stared.

The chamber was a big cavern, but it was already filled with riches.

They were heaped around the prince's burial casket – piles of gold, silver and precious gemstones.

They sparkled like the sea in the early morning.

Then Napoleon saw Haprall being led to a stone bench that was raised above the crowd.

Temple helpers lifted him up and sat him on the bench. The High Priest poured a dark liquid from a golden jug into a silver goblet.

'That is a special sleeping drink,' said Skin. 'The boy will not wake up from it.'

'You mean it's poison?' gasped Napoleon.

'Affirmative,' said Skin. 'It slows down the nervous system.'

The High Priest handed the goblet to Haprall. He took it, and raised it to his lips.

'**Stop!**' Napoleon shouted. 'Don't drink. **It's poison**.'

Haprall lifted his eyes in surprise, and the mourners turned.

'Seize the boy,' commanded the High Priest. 'How dare he interrupt the funeral procession.'

Napoleon tried to scramble up to Haprall, but he was dragged down. The priest pointed a bony finger at him.

'Be patient, boy,' he said. 'Your turn to sip the elixir of sleep will come soon enough.'

He turned back to Haprall. 'Drink, and prepare for your journey.'

Napoleon tried to call out, but a rough hand across his mouth stifled his words. He watched helplessly as Haprall raised the goblet to his lips once more.

CHAPTER TEN

'**STOP!**'

A voice of authority echoed through the chamber. It was King Muwatalli.

'Put the goblet down,' he told Haprall.

'But Great One,' the High Priest said.

The king silenced him.

'Is this not the Battle Boy I heard spoken of in the city streets? The boy who brought us luck? I want to hear what he has to say,' Muwatalli boomed, turning his gaze on Napoleon. 'Release him.'

Napoleon was freed at once.

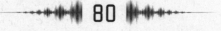

'What is this you say about the elixir of sleep?'

'It is poison, my king,' said Napoleon.

'He knows nothing of these matters, Great One,' the priest muttered. 'The elixir is given by the gods to bring on the sleep needed for the journey to the Land of Darkness.'

'The sleep you talk of is nothing but death,' said Napoleon. 'And that drink is just a poison that kills.'

'How dare you!' the High Priest shouted, striking at Napoleon with his sceptre. 'It is a great honour to go with the prince to the place of eternal sleep.'

'Well, if it's such a great honour,' Napoleon replied, 'why don't you go with him?'

The priest was silent.

'Well?' said King Muwatalli. 'What have you to say, Wise One?'

The priest stood with his mouth wide open.

Muwatalli helped Haprall down from the stone bench and took the goblet away.

'You are free,' the king said. 'Both of you. Thanks to you, Battle Boy, we won a great victory today.'

'But the prince must be accompanied on his journey,' the High Priest insisted.

'And he will be.' Muwatalli stared down at the goblet, then at the priest. 'And I think I know who should have that *great honour*.'

'I like your king,' Napoleon said to Haprall as they walked away from the tomb of Prince Terrepas.

'But isn't he your king as well?' said Haprall.

'No. I come from somewhere else, far away.'

'I thought so. Are you a messenger from the gods?'

'Kind of.' Napoleon could hear the professor telling him that the Exit Beam was ready. 'And soon I have to go again, this time forever.'

'You came to bring us luck in our battle with the pharaoh.'

'Well, sort of. And I brought you luck in the tomb.'

Haprall wrinkled his brow. 'Perhaps.'

'I thought I saved your life,' said Napoleon.

'You did. And for that I thank you. But . . .'

'But what?'

'I would have stayed there, gladly. I would have drunk the elixir to accompany the prince forever.'

'But why?' said Napoleon.

'To protect my prince and his tomb. Robbers will come one day and steal it all. I hate that thought. Prince Terrepas was a great Hittite warrior, and he should be left to rest in peace. If I stayed I would have helped make sure of that. But now . . . '

Napoleon thought about all the treasures in the tomb. They would buy a ton of iPods and Playstations, heaps of games and books and buckets of burgers and chips and loads of lollies, plus squillions of skateboards and scooters, skycatchers and . . .

OPERATION BB
$millionkid

But then he looked at Haprall's sad face. 'Don't worry,' Napoleon said after a while. 'Your prince is safe in his tomb. Robbers will never find it. The gods have told me.'

Napoleon glanced down at his Battle Watch and fiddled with its dials. That should fix things, he said to himself as a DELETE sign flashed across the screen.

'It makes me so happy to hear you say this,' Haprall said. 'You are a true friend. But I think we must part now.' Haprall pointed to a shaft of light near the city wall. 'The gods are calling for you.'

'You're right,' said Napoleon. He shook Haprall's hand in Hittite style, clasping each others forearm, then turned and walked towards the Exit Beam.

When he reached the beam, Professor Perdu's voice came through loud and clear.

'Just checking, BB005. You do have the coordinates for the tomb, don't you?'

'Tomb?' Napoleon said as he stepped into the beam. 'What tomb?'

The lost tomb of Prince Terrepas is shrouded in mystery. Many archaeologists say that the tomb doesn't even exist. Perhaps the prince is just a character from my imagination? Whatever the case, it is certainly one of the great mysteries of history.

Charlie Carter

VAMPIRE VIRUS

A GIRL?

Battle Boy 005 can't believe it!

Professor Perdu is sending him on a mission with a Battle Girl — BG001.

She's a virus expert. And a know-it-all.

Their mission is to **find and destroy** the virus dracs that are sucking the life out of the Battle Books.

One bossy Battle Girl + hundreds of angry dracs =

Battle Boy's toughest mission yet.

Battle Boy 005 is hurtling through time.
Destination: 1587

It's his very first mission for Operation Battle Book!

He's supposed to land on Sir Francis Drake's ship.

But the GC-Locator isn't working properly.

So BB makes a big splash and skis onto a wave – into a fierce battle between English and Spanish warships.

The professor orders him to exit ASAP.

But BB005 has other plans . . .

Battle Boy is in the wrong place at the wrong time.

He's supposed to be finding out who shot down the Red Baron – the most famous pilot of World War One.

Instead he has to convince a trigger-happy sergeant that he's not a spy.

Then he has to outrun a German jeep called a Torpedo on a rickety old motorbike!

And this is before the mission has even begun . . .

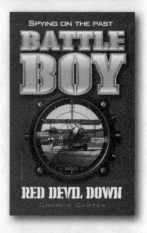

Keep your head down, Battle Boy!

Arrows are flying, fireballs are scorching the sky, soldiers are hurling spears and clashing swords – BB005 has landed in the middle of a battle between the Greeks and the Trojans.

His mission: to find out if the Greeks really left the Trojan Horse outside the gates of the city.

But then Battle Boy meets Polyxena, King Priam's daughter.

Can he save Polly and finish his mission?

Battle Boy 005 is spinning through time.
Destination: Dark Age England 954.

He's in trouble as soon as he lands.

Villagers from the Dark Ages don't like boys who fall from the sky. Neither does Bloodaxe, the fierce Viking King of York. He makes Battle Boy fight his son, Haeric.

Luckily, BB005 has the latest version of Viking FightRite to help him out.

But he's going to need a lot more than that when he gets caught up in a **time twister!**

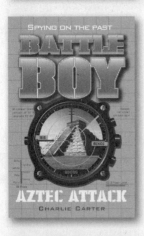

There's something fishy about this mission.

Battle Boy 005 is dressed as a big bird — but that's not it.

There's something Professor Perdu isn't telling him.

Why does he have more gadgets than ever before?

Why is Skin scanning the faces of all the Aztecs and Spaniards?

Who are they looking for?

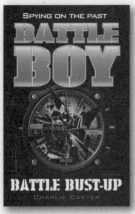

BATTLE BOY ALERT:

Top Secret Mission ahead.

Two battles have become entangled in the same Battle Book.

Battle Boy 005 has to dodge tanks and chariots, spears and bullets, and convince Alexander the Great he's not a Persian spy.

He needs Professor Perdu's **most secret** invention for this mission:

the BEK.